THE DOG WHO HAD KITTENS

THE DOG WHO HAD KITTENS

by Polly M. Robertus
illustrated by Janet Stevens

Holiday House / New York

For all my parents
P.R.

This story first appeared in *Cricket, The Magazine for Children*,
March 1988 volume 15, number 7.

Library of Congress Cataloging-in-Publication Data

Robertus, Polly M.
The dog who had kittens / by Polly M. Robertus ;
illustrated by Janet Stevens.—1st ed.
p.   cm.
''This story first appeared in Cricket, the magazine for
children, March 1988, volume 15, number 7''—Verso t.p.
Summary: Baxter the Basset Hound comes to the aid of
some kittens when their mother disappears one afternoon.
ISBN 0-8234-0860-4
[1. Dogs—Fiction. 2. Cats—Fiction.] I. Stevens, Janet, ill.
II. Title.
PZ7.R5515Do 1991
[E]—dc20   90-39174   CIP   AC
ISBN 0-8234-0974-0 (pbk.)

Baxter the Basset Hound was in his backyard enjoying the smells of spring. Suddenly, he heard a fuss. "Eloise!" the boy was shouting. "Everybody, come look at Eloise!" Baxter trotted toward the side of the garage.

He got there just as the boy's parents did. He had to push his head between all the legs to see what was going on. There, lying on her side in a box, was Eloise. When she saw Baxter, she bristled her fur and hissed.

Baxter just had time to see the squirming little bodies attached to her belly before the boy led him away to the oak tree.

"You'd better stay here for awhile," said the boy. "We're going to move Eloise into the house with the kittens. She's very nervous."

So Baxter was chained to the tree and abandoned.

Kittens! he thought. Just what I need, more cats around the
place. More attention for Eloise! Less attention for me!
He lifted his head and howled.

Hours went by. No one even looked at him. It was almost dinnertime when, to his surprise, Eloise herself came toward him from the house.

"Congratulations," he said as sincerely as he could.

Eloise was licking a paw. "Marvelous, aren't they?" she purred.

"How many?"

"Seven. Three of them look like me. Gorgeous."

Baxter slumped down in the grass. Seven kittens! This was worse than he'd imagined. "That's nice," he said miserably. "How long am I going to be an outcast, then?"

"It wasn't my idea to chain you up. All the same, I'd appreciate it if you'd stay away for awhile. You are a dog, and the kittens and I are cats. I know you for a very good fellow, but I must warn you: Don't come near my kittens!" And she stalked off toward the house.

Finally the boy fed Baxter and scratched and hugged him.
But the ball didn't come out, and Baxter wasn't invited for a
walk. Worst of all, Baxter had to go to bed in the garage.

It went on like that for three days.

Baxter was allowed in the house, but not in the laundry room, where the kittens lay in a large box. He could hear their thin cries from time to time.

One day the family left the house, but didn't quite shut the laundry-room door. Baxter nosed it open and pushed inside. He could hear the kittens crying. Eloise was nowhere in sight.

Baxter hung his head over the side of the box and had a good look. Suddenly he didn't feel a bit jealous. They're so tiny, he thought. Their eyes aren't open, and they can't even hold their little heads up or walk. The mewing babies seemed to be searching. Their cries were the most pitiful sounds Baxter had ever heard.

Suddenly Baxter was furious with Eloise. Where was she? What right had she to leave her babies alone like this? When had they last eaten? Baxter began to pace around the room. The kittens' cries grew louder. Oh, why, why doesn't anyone come, he thought desperately.

Finally he went back to the box. The kittens were in a ball in one corner. Delicately, Baxter stepped into the box. He lay down carefully, taking most of the extra space. The kittens sensed his warmth and began to pull themselves toward him, crying louder than ever. Blindly they stumbled and tumbled over each other until they were between his front paws.

Little muzzles scouted his fur, little mouths sucked at his legs and neck, little paws with needles massaged him. Baxter was afraid to move for fear of crushing one of them. He held still for a long time. At last the kittens fell asleep. He sniffed and poked them gently with his big nose.

All at once he felt happier than he'd
ever felt before. I did it! he thought. I
helped them. They feel safe now. This
is wonderful!

Suddenly there was Eloise, with eyes
like embers. Eloise gave him a hard
look, leaped into the box and began at
once to sniff and push the kittens. They
began to waken and cry. ''Get out,''
Eloise said.

Baxter climbed carefully out of the box. "I didn't hurt them."

"I can see that. But it's feeding time. You're in the way."

"Past feeding time!" Baxter said, remembering his anger. "Poor little mites, crying and crying. And where were you, then?"

"None of your business. And don't think I don't know *my* business. Kittens are always hungry, they think. I have to get away from time to time."

Baxter looked at Eloise. The kittens were suckling. "A pretty sight," he said humbly.

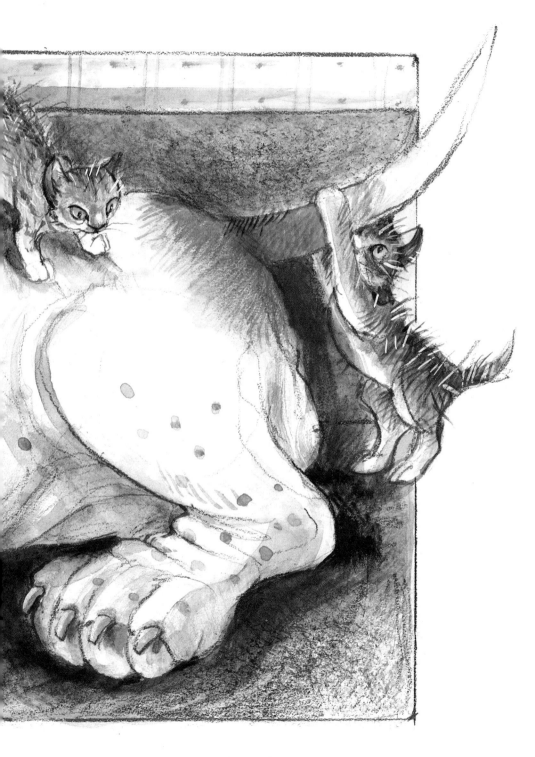

Once the family realized that Eloise trusted Baxter around the kittens, everyone relaxed. He could come and go as he liked. To everyone's surprise, he spent most of his time with the kittens. Since Eloise only came around to feed and wash her babies, it was Baxter who really took care of them. The kittens seemed to think of his nose, tail, and especially his long, dangling ears, as a kitten playground.

Baxter was with the kittens when they opened their eyes and when they began to walk. When they first learned how to climb out of the box, he nearly went crazy trying to keep track of them.

He'd forgotten about his old life until one day, when the kittens were several weeks old, the boy came downstairs whistling and tossing a ball. "Come on, Baxter, let's go to the field," he called. Baxter, suddenly remembering old times, ran outside and trotted happily alongside the bicycle. They played fetch and then went into the woods nearby. Baxter dug up a rotting catcher's mitt and, to his joy, the boy let him keep it.

When Baxter got home, he lay down and gave his mitt a thorough chew. Out of the corner of his eye, he saw Eloise vanishing through her cat door. Suddenly, he remembered the kittens!

Baxter raced to the house, nosed open the door, and skidded across the kitchen linoleum, into the laundry room.

The box was empty! Sniffing, Baxter searched for the kittens, but he couldn't find a single one. Neither could he hear them. Where, oh, where could they be?

He sat down and howled.

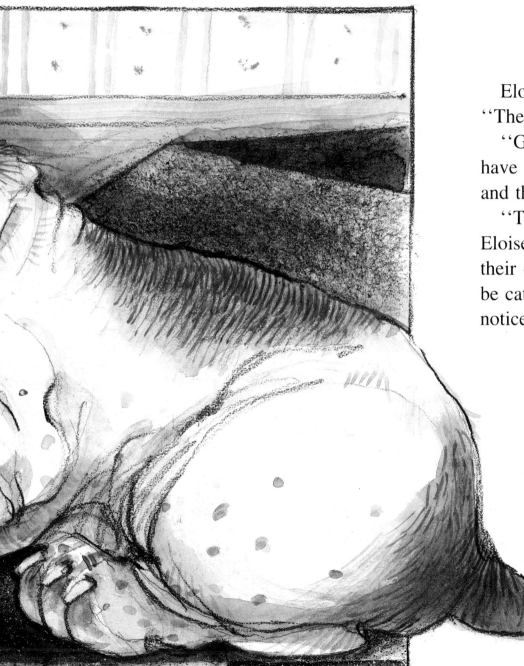

Eloise and the boy appeared. "They're gone, of course," Eloise said.

"Gone? Where? Where could they have gone? I leave them for one day, and they vanish!" said Baxter.

"They don't need us anymore," Eloise said. "They've got homes of their own now, where they've gone to be cats, like me. Goodness, didn't you notice how big they were getting?"

Baxter could hardly eat his food that night. He lay at the boy's feet after dinner, and when the family went to bed he tried to sleep, but he just felt too lonely.

Finally he got up and went into the laundry room, where the box was full of moonlight. He snuggled up in it, comforted by its kitten smell. He was still feeling too sad to sleep when, with a soft thud, Eloise landed next to him and curled up by his head.

"It occurs to me, I never did thank you for all your help,"
she said.

"You're welcome. I enjoyed every minute of it," he sniffed.

Eloise began absently to lick his ear. "Well," she said, "I
have to admit, it's strange without them. It's good to know I
might have more kittens—someday. Anyway, I'm glad you're
still here."

"Oh Eloise, really?" Baxter sighed happily. He fell asleep at
last while Eloise licked and licked his ear, just as though it were
a kitten.